Dear Parents:

Congratulations! Your child is taking the first steps on an exciting journey. The destination? Independent reading!

STEP INTO READING® will help your child get there. The program offers five steps to reading success. Each step includes fun stories and colorful art or photographs. In addition to original fiction and books with favorite characters, there are Step into Reading Non-Fiction Readers, Phonics Readers and Boxed Sets, Sticker Readers, and Comic Readers—a complete literacy program with something to interest every child.

Learning to Read, Step by Step!

Ready to Read   Preschool–Kindergarten
• big type and easy words • rhyme and rhythm • picture clues
For children who know the alphabet and are eager to begin reading.

Reading with Help   Preschool–Grade 1
• basic vocabulary • short sentences • simple stories
For children who recognize familiar words and sound out new words with help.

Reading on Your Own   Grades 1–3
• engaging characters • easy-to-follow plots • popular topics
For children who are ready to read on their own.

Reading Paragraphs   Grades 2–3
• challenging vocabulary • short paragraphs • exciting stories
For newly independent readers who read simple sentences with confidence.

Ready for Chapters   Grades 2–4
• chapters • longer paragraphs • full-color art
For children who want to take the plunge into chapter books but still like colorful pictures.

STEP INTO READING® is designed to give every child a successful reading experience. The grade levels are only guides; children will progress through the steps at their own speed, developing confidence in their reading.

Remember, a lifetime love of reading starts with a single step!

Welcome to Builder Cove!
Rubble and his family
live here.
They love to build.

Rubble is a leader.

He drives a bulldozer.

Rubble also loves
to play.

Rubble solves problems.
He shows the crew
what to do.

Meet Mix!

She is very smart.

She loves
to paint.

Charger drives
a crane.
It has a grabber!

Zoom, zoom!

Charger is fast.

Wheeler keeps things
very clean.

He moves

wood and bricks

in his dump truck.

Motor is small,
but she is strong.
She can smash stuff.
Boom!

Grandpa Gravel

helps the pups.

Auntie Crane

helps, too!

Mayor Greatway

is in charge of

Builder Cove.

Oh, no!

Her ceiling is cracking.

She needs help!

Rubble and his crew
are ready!

They work together.

They fix the roof.

Rubble and the crew
to the rescue!